Reading Together

THE TRUE STORY OF
HUMPTY
DUMPTY

D1312263

Read it together

It's never too early to share books with children. Reading together is a wonderful way for your child to enjoy books and stories— and learn to read!

One of the most important ways of helping your child learn to read is by reading aloud— either rereading their favorite books, or getting to know new ones.

Encourage your child to join in with the reading in every possible way. They may be able to talk about the pictures, point to the words, take over parts of the reading, or retell the story afterward.

With books they know well, children can try reading to you. Don't worry if the words aren't always the same as the words on the page.

If they are reading and get stuck on a word, show them how to guess what it says by:
* looking at the pictures
* looking at the letter the word begins with
* reading the rest of the sentence and coming back to it.
Always help them out if they get really stuck or tired.

Sometimes you can help children look more closely at the actual words and letters. See if they can find words they recognize, or letters from their name. Help them write some of the words they know.

Talk about books with them and discuss the stories and pictures. Compare new books with ones they already know.

We hope you enjoy reading this book together.

Text copyright © 1987 by Sarah Hayes
Illustrations copyright © 1987 by Charlotte Voake
Introductory and concluding notes copyright © by 1998 CLPE/L B Southwark

Second U.S. edition in this form 1999

Library of Congress Catalog Card Number 98-88097

ISBN 0-7636-0864-5

4 6 8 10 9 7 5

Printed in Hong Kong

Candlewick Press
2067 Massachusetts Avenue
Cambridge, Massachusetts 02140

THE TRUE STORY OF HUMPTY DUMPTY

Sarah Hayes
illustrated by Charlotte Voake

CANDLEWICK PRESS

Humpty Dumpty sat on a wall.
A horse came up to watch.
"Can you sit on this wall, horse?"
Humpty Dumpty said.

"Of course," said the horse.
And he did.

Then he wobbled and wobbled,
and then he fell off.

Humpty Dumpty laughed.
"Tee-hee," he said,
"you've hurt your knee."

Humpty Dumpty sat on the wall.
Another horse came up to watch.
"Can you stand on this wall, horse?"
Humpty Dumpty said.

"Of course," said the horse.
And he did.

Then he wobbled and wobbled,
and then he fell off.

Humpty Dumpty laughed.
"Oh dear," he said,
"you've hurt your ear."

Humpty Dumpty sat on the wall.
A man came up to watch.
"Can you stand on one leg
on this wall, man?"
Humpty Dumpty said.

"Yes," said the man, "I can."
And he did.

Then he wobbled and wobbled,
and then he fell off.

Humpty Dumpty laughed.
"Ho-ho," he said,
"you've hurt your toe."

Humpty Dumpty sat on the wall.
Another man came up to watch.
"Can you stand on one leg
and juggle with bricks
on this wall, man?"
Humpty Dumpty said.

"Well," said the man,
"I think I can."
 And he did.

Then he wobbled and wobbled,
and then he fell off.

Humpty Dumpty laughed.
"Go to bed," he said,
"you've hurt your head."

Humpty Dumpty sat on the wall.
The king came up to watch.
He saw his horses
and he saw his men.

And the king was terribly,
terribly annoyed.

"Come down," the king said.
"Come down from that wall."
But Humpty Dumpty said nothing at all.
He stood on one leg and juggled with bricks.
He did cartwheels and headstands
and all sorts of tricks.

Then he wobbled and wobbled,
and then he fell off.
CRASH!

And all the king's horses

and all the king's men . . .

put Humpty Dumpty together again.
And Humpty said, "After such a great fall,
I'll never ever climb back on that wall."

But he did!

Read it again

The true story?

A good way to help children see the jokes in *The True Story of Humpty Dumpty* is to read them the original rhyme. What differences do they notice?

Ashes!

Ashes!

We all hop around.

> *Humpty Dumpty sat on a wall,*
> *Humpty Dumpty had a great fall.*
> *All the king's horses and all the king's men*
> *Couldn't put Humpty together again.*

Different endings

This story changes a well-known rhyme and has a different ending. You could make up your own endings to other familiar rhymes, such as "Jack and Jill," "Little Jack Horner," "Ring-around-the-Roses," and "Hey Diddle, Diddle."

Talking pictures

Using the pictures in the book, children can retell the story in their own words.

The horse sat on the wall and ate some of Humpty Dumpty's cupcakes.

Humpty Dumpty sat on a wall.
A horse came up to watch.
"Can you sit on this wall, horse?"
Humpty Dumpty said.

"Of course," said the horse.
And he did.

Then he wobbled and wobbled.
and then he fell off.

Act it out

This story is a good one to act out using toys or puppets with an imaginary wall, such as a chair seat or an upturned box.

Make a tape

You can read the book together and make a tape of it for your child to play back with the book.

Humpty Dumpty laughed.
"Tee-hee," he said.
"you've hurt your knee."

Different versions

There are lots of different versions of "Humpty Dumpty" you could find in nursery rhyme collections and in stories like these. Look for *Once Upon a Time*—another Reading Together story— which includes Humpty Dumpty and other familiar characters, such as the Three Bears and Little Red Riding Hood.

Reading Together

The Reading Together series is divided into four levels—starting with red, then on to yellow, blue, and finally green. The six books in each level offer children varied experiences of reading. There are stories, poems, rhymes and songs, traditional tales, and information books to choose from.

Accompanying the series is the *Reading Together Parents' Handbook,* which looks at all the different ways children learn to read and explains how *your* help can really make a difference!